Icy Magic
Catlyn the Clownfish Fairy

BY
AANYA GARG

Pharos Books

Paperback ISBN
9789355464224

©Publisher

Publisher: Pharos Books (P) Ltd.
Plot No.-55, Main Mother Dairy Road
Pandav Nagar, East Delhi-110092
Phone: 011-40395855, +14049995474
WhatsApp: +91 8368220032
E-mail: sales@pharosbooks.in
Website: www.pharosbooks.in
First Edition: 2022

Printed By: Sushma Book Binding House, Okhla
Industrial Area, Phase II, New Delhi-110020

Icy Magic: Catlyn the Clownfish Fairy
Aanya Garg

Books in Icy Magic Series

Ocean Fairies

Oceana the Ocean fairy

Anna the Anglerfish fairy

Sophia the Stonefish fairy

Olivia the Octopus fairy

Catlyn the Clownfish fairy

Rosella the Rockfish fairy

Molly the Manatee fairy

Dedicated to

My Grandma and Grandpa

(Mrs. Shipra Garg Dr. S.K. Garg)
You have always been cheering me on and
encouraging me in whatever hobbies
I put my hand to.
I love you!

CONTENTS

Each of the seven ocean fairies has a magical shell to keep the oceans in order. But Fireblast, a squawker, had stolen all the shells to create chaos in the oceans. The ocean fairies' powers are limited in the human world, that is why they took the help of two girls, Alice and Christy, to help them recover the shells. By placing their hands on a fairy when needed, the fairy's power increases. Thus far, only four shells have been found out of seven.

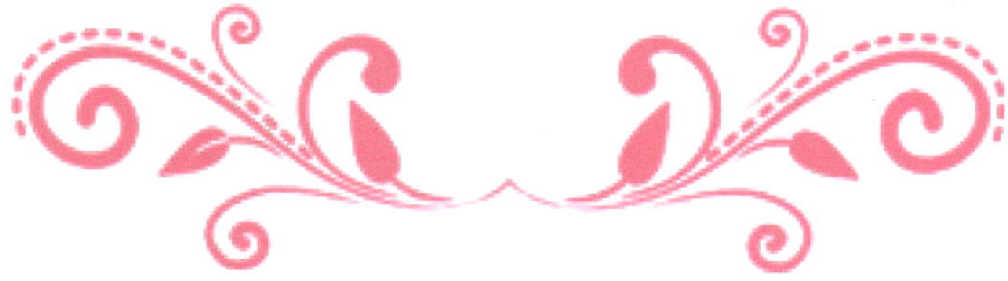

CHAPTER 1

Coral Blue Adventures had set up camp at Coral Beach. It was time for snorkeling on the eighth day at the camp. Each kid was given a pair

of snorkeling goggles and a life jacket to explore
underwater life.

Alice and Christy were snorkeling together.
While they were enjoying the underwater action,
they were amazed to see shoals of fish near some
whitish corals zooming away from them despite
the fish food thrown at them.

Then some orange corals at a distance, sparkling and glowing brightly, caught their eye. They swam near the orange corals. There they saw Catlyn, the Clownfish Fairy, hovering out of the corals waving to them. She made hand gestures indicating her need for help.

The girls, who were on a secret mission to help the fairies, nodded to Catlyn. Catlyn gave a thankful smile and waved her wand. A handful of sparkling fairy dust fell on the girls, dwindling them down to the size of a fairy. Pink wings unfurled from their backs lifting them into the air. They found themselves hovering above the Atlantic Ocean.

"**P**lease tell us what's happening and how can we help this time," said Alice and Christy. Catlyn waved her wand in the air and an outline of a clown fish appeared in the sky with a picture formed inside.

It showed a flashback of Fireblast sneakily boarding a ship and talking to himself.

"Finally, I am able to keep this shell for a longer time, if not forever, while enjoying the ride." It showed him sitting on a recliner in the

balcony of his room on a ten-storey ship, facing the sea and misusing Catlyn's shell to heat up the ocean water. Fireblast had a lot of fun seeing how all the animals were searching for other places to live in as their homes got heated up. He laughed gleefully.

Catlyn explained sadly that without the amethyst shell, she would not be able to keep the rising ocean temperature in check. "If ocean temperature rises, the corals will start bleaching and even die. Rising temperatures and dying corals will force sea animals and fishes to migrate in search for more favorable habitats. Many ocean animals who are sensitive to even small changes in temperature will become dangerously sick and might also die. There will also be more hurricanes. All of this will further impact human life. Humans are dependent on fish for their food and livelihood. Everything will be chaotic. We need to find the ruby shell quickly"

CHAPTER
3

Christy and Alice were eager to help Catlyn find her shell. They recalled sighting whitish corals while they were snorkeling and now could relate why the distressed fishes zoomed away from the food. They quickly made a plan. "Let's get on that

ship," said Alice. With a wave of Catlyn's wand, they snuck aboard the ship.

When nobody was looking, Catlyn turned girls back to their original size and disguised Christy as a food service person. Then, drawing on energy from the girls' contact, the fairy created a magical potion.

Fireblast had ordered hot chocolate with marshmallows and pizza. Taking advantage of that, Christy pushed a food trolley to his room. She rang the doorbell. Fireblast opened the door.

Christy greeted him and moved the food trolley into the room and left. Alice and Catlyn were hiding under the food trolley.

CHAPTER 4

After Fireblast took a sip of his hot chocolate, he sprang into a headstand position and the amethyst shell in his pocket dropped on the floor with a clink.

Fireblast did not know that the fairy had mixed a headstand potion in his drink. He tried his hardest to get back on his feet but it seemed as if his head was glued fast to the floor. Catlyn and Alice shot out from their hiding place, laughing at him and grabbing the shell. Fireblast got a glimpse

of the fairy, "YOU!" He shot heat rays at them, but they dodged it quickly.

Since the magic of the headstand potion could only last for a few minutes as fairy power waned quickly in the human world, they rushed out of the room and joined Christy, who was waiting for them right outside.

Catlyn waved her wand and this time they landed in Icy Palace before the King and Queen. Catlyn handed the shell to them. The Queen kept the shell safely back in the treasure box. She was happy that Catlyn was able to get her shell back from Fireblast. Thankfully all the animals and corals were out of danger. The queen thanked the two girls, "Icy Palace is grateful for your help. Once again you have shown us your bravery and proven that you are the fairies' best friends."

Catlyn hugged Alice and Christy. Then she swung her wand and whispered a spell. With a flick of the wand, the girls were back in the human world.

Alice and Christy managed to find five shells but three are still missing. What will be their next adventure? Which shell will they find next? Read on in the next book Rosella the Rockfish Fairy.

What are Corals?

- Corals may look like rocks or colourful plants attached to the seafloor, but they are actually small animals living together in large groups called colonies. These animals are called polyps and each coral polyp is only a few millimetres long.
- All the polyps in a colony are genetically identical. They stay permanently in one place attached to a rock.
- A coral polyp begins its life as a tiny, free-swimming larva, which is only the size of the head of a pin. It settles on a rock or hard surface and never moves again.
- Each polyp builds a case of limestone skeleton around itself, using calcium from the water. It is like a house with a floor and walls. This limestone skeleton remains even after the polyp dies and forms a foundation for another polyp to build a house on, putting a floor on the roof of the old polyp.
- An enormous limestone formation made of and by millions of polyps is called coral reef. The outside layer of a reef is alive. The inside layers of a reef are made of the skeletons of dead coral, some of which lived millions of years ago.

What is Coral Bleaching?

- Coral bleaching happens when corals lose their vibrant colours and turn white. Corals, otherwise translucent, appear bright and colourful because of the microscopic algae that live in their tissue.
- Algae live within corals in a mutually beneficial relationship, each helping the other survive. Corals provide algae a protected place to live in, and in return algae supply corals with the food and oxygen they need to survive.
- When the ocean environment changes—if it gets too hot, for instance— corals stress out and expel the algae. As the algae leave, the corals fade, eventually acquiring a bleached appearance.
- Bleached corals are not dead, but are more at risk of starvation and disease. If the temperature stays high for a long time, the corals won't let the algae back and the coral will die.
- An increase in temperature of just one degree Celsius for only four weeks can trigger bleaching. Corals may bleach for other reasons: extremely low tides, pollution, or too much sunlight.

WORD SEARCH

```
I  M  C  S  R  F  X  S  A  P  M  K
F  Q  V  O  G  X  K  Y  M  I  I  O
N  M  R  A  R  K  J  X  E  P  G  B
C  B  S  Q  L  A  C  C  T  G  R  G
A  Y  S  S  L  O  L  X  H  Q  A  M
S  N  O  R  K  E  L  A  Y  B  T  I
H  D  B  R  B  R  F  T  S  A  E  P
C  A  T  L  Y  N  G  H  T  J  A  K
```

1. Coral   2. Amethyst   3. Snorkel

4. Migrate   5. Catlyn

My special thanks to:

My aunt Pratiksha and uncle Archit for their enthusiastic support and reading through my manuscripts numerous times and offering detailed, helpful advice.

My editor, Li Ping, who edited my books with her usual fine eye to details. Her expertise and advice have been invaluable.

My illustrator, Aru, who designed my book with patience and panache and rendered amazing book cover and illustrations.

Released Already!

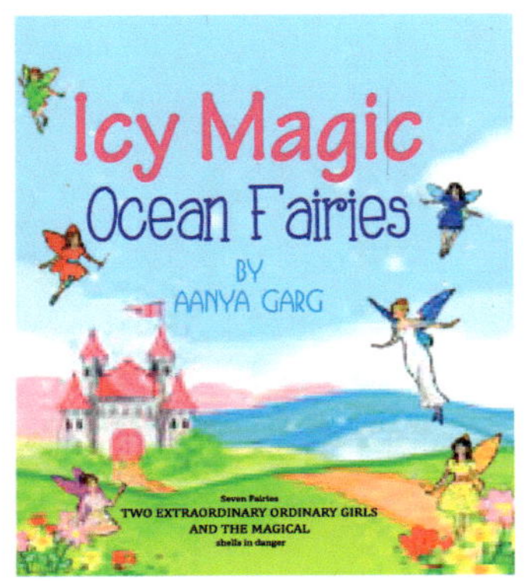  

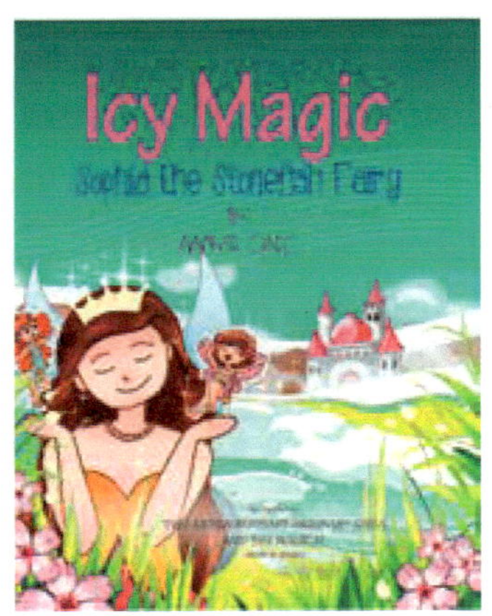 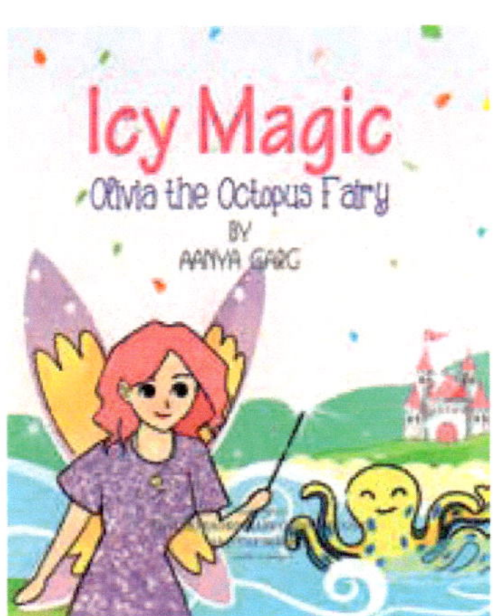 

Next book in Icy Magic series
Rosella the Rockfish fairy

Made in the USA
Monee, IL
07 July 2026

56552323R00019